Come with me

Holly M. McGhee

illustrated by Pascal Lemaître

G. P. PUTNAM'S SONS

G. P. PUTNAM'S SONS
an imprint of Penguin Random House LLC
375 Hudson Street
New York, NY 10014

Library of Congress Cataloging-in-Publication Data is available upon request.
Printed in the United States of America.
ISBN 9781524739058
3 5 7 9 10 8 6 4

Book design and title lettering by Jaclyn Reyes.
Text set in Burgstaedt Antiqua Com.
The art for this book was created with ink and watercolor.

Come With Me is written in honor of friendship,
bravery, and the fact that we aren't powerless,
no matter how small and insignificant we may feel.

—Holly & Pascal

*". . . though at the level of the individual
our actions are as light as a cloud,
united they can change the color of the sky."*

—Yvette Pierpaoli,

REFUGEES INTERNATIONAL

All over the world,
the news told
and told
and retold
of anger and hatred—

People against people.

And the little girl was frightened
by everything she heard
and saw
and felt.

She asked her papa
if there was something
she could do
to make the world a better place.

Her papa said,

"Come with me."

Hand in hand they walked out the door
to the subway.

Waiting there on the platform,
her papa tipped his hat
to those he met.

So the little girl
did, too.

They rode the train
through the tunnels
underground.

The girl and her papa were brave and kind,
and that day
they won a tiny battle
over fear
for themselves
and for the people of the world.

The news kept telling of anger and hatred.

And the little girl asked her mama
what she could do
to make the world a better place.

Her mama said,
"Come with me."

They went to their grocery
to buy some things for dinner—

because one person
doesn't represent a family
or a race
or the people of a land.

Her mama cooked,
and the girl set the table,
piece by piece,
as she'd always done.

Plate in the middle.
Knife and spoon to the right.
Fork on the left,
napkin by its side.
Water glass.

The little girl sat
with her mama and her papa,
and they ate together.

Her dog nuzzled her
under the table.
She scratched his head.

"I want to do something of my own,"
she said. "Can I walk the dog?"

Her parents looked at each other,
and they looked at their child.

They let her go,
and sent a message to the world.

They would not live in fear.

And when the little girl
opened the door,
the boy
across the hall
opened his door, too.

"Where are you going?" he asked.

The little girl said,
"Come with me."

Because two people together
are stronger
than one.

The girl, the boy, and the dog
were happy
to be out.

One step
at a time,
they understood
what they could do
to make the world
a better place.

They could go on.

Brave, gentle, strong—
and kind . . .

to one another

and all living things.

As tiny as it was,
their part mattered to the world.

Your part matters, too.

Come with me.